W9-BPL-150
5 0508 01930 138 2

Super Ben's Brave Bike Ride:

A Book About Courage

by Shelley Marshall Illustrated by Ben Mahan

Super Ben wants to be brave. Being brave is when you do something you are afraid to do. Help Ben get to Molly the Great's. **Let's read!**

Enslow Elementary
an imprint of

Enslow Publishers, Inc.
40 Industrial Road
Box 398
Berkeley Heights, NJ 07922
USA
http://www.enslow.com

“Hi, Ben,” says Molly. “Can you come over and play?”

“I’ll ask my mom,” says Ben.

“Mom, can I go to Molly’s?”

“Not right now. I must wait for Nana. I will take you later.”

Ben does not want to wait. What can he do?

“I have an idea!” Ben shouts.

"What if?" says Ben.

Ben's idea is so big. Can he really do it?

Ben gets his cape. He gets his helmet.

“What if I go to Molly’s by myself? I can ride my bike!”

“What a super idea! You are a super bike rider!” says Mom.

"Bye Ben! Have fun!" Mom calls.

Ben holds on with both paws. He keeps his head up.

“1, 2, 3.” Ben counts the houses. His tummy feels a little funny. But he does not turn around.

"4, 5." Ben's paws are sweaty. But he keeps going.

"6." Ben sees Molly's building. His heart beats fast. Can he really do it?

"I did it! I was brave!" cheers Ben.

"Good job, Ben!" Mom and Nana shout.

Read More About Being Brave

Books

Hirschmann, Kris. *Courage*. Chicago: Raintree, 2004.

Keller, Kristin Thoennes. *Courage*. Mankato, MN: Capstone Press, 2005.

Web Site

Kids Next Door
www.hud.gov/kids/people.html

Enslow Elementary, an imprint of Enslow Publishers, Inc.

Library of Congress Cataloging-in-Publication Data

Marshall, Shelley, 1968-
Super Ben's brave bike ride : a book about courage / Shelley Marshall.
p. cm. — (Character education with Super Ben and Molly the Great)
ISBN 978-0-7660-3515-7
1. Courage in children—Juvenile literature. 2. Courage—Juvenile literature. I. Title.
BF723.C694M37 2010
179'.6—dc22
2008052625

ISBN-13: 978-0-7660-3740-3 (paperback edition)

Printed in the United States of America

112009 Lake Book Manufacturing, Inc., Melrose Park, IL

10 9 8 7 6 5 4 3 2 1

To Our Readers: We have done our best to make sure all Internet Addresses in this book were active and appropriate when we went to press. However, the author and the publisher have no control and assume no liability for the material available on those Internet sites or on other Web sites they may link to. Any comments or suggestions can be sent by e-mail to comments@enslow.com or to the address on the back cover.

Enslow Publishers, Inc. is committed to printing our books on recycled paper. The paper in every book contains 10% to 30% post-consumer waste (PCW). The cover board on the outside of every book contains 100% PCW. Our goal is to do our part to help young people and the environment too!